DEDICATIONS

Fabienne:
For Papa Fito and Maman Titine.

J:
To my greatest loves: David, Alejandro, and Annalise.

www.LilLibros.com

Love is Still Winning / El amor siempre triunfa
Published by Little Libros, LLC

Text © 2024 Fabienne Doucet
Art © 2024 Little Libros, LLC
Art by J de laVega
Cover Designed by Ana Godinez
Designed by Haydeé Yañez

Library of Congress Control Number: 2023941618

Printed in China

First Edition – 2024 JHP 03/24
28 27 26 25 24   1 2 3 4 5
ISBN: 978-1-948066-11-2

Love is Still Winning

EL AMOR SIEMPRE TRIUNFA

story by Fabienne Doucet
art by J de laVega

Lil' LIBROS

When I came into the kitchen this morning, Mama was reading the newspaper. She had tears in her eyes.

Cuando entré a la cocina esta mañana,
Mamá estaba leyendo el periódico.
Tenía lágrimas en los ojos.

"Why are you crying, Mama?"

"I was reading a sad story about people saying mean things to others because of what they look like, where they come from, and what they believe in."

"¿Por qué lloras, Mamá?".

"Estaba leyendo una historia triste sobre algunas personas que dicen cosas feas sobre otras personas, solo por su apariencia, por el lugar de donde vienen y por sus creencias".

"Why would they do that, Mama? Don't they know we should be kind to one another? Don't they want new friends?"
"Oh, my little one," she said. "Those are good questions. I wish I knew the answers."

"¿Por qué harían eso, Mamá? ¿No saben que debemos ser amables con los demás? ¿No quieren nuevos amigos?".
"Ay, mi chiquitin", dijo Mamá. "Son buenas preguntas. Ojalá supiera las respuestas".

I thought and thought for a while, then I told Mama, "I have an idea! Maybe we should remind them that love is everywhere!"
"What do you mean?" she asked curiously.
"I mean, that love is still *winning*, Mama! I see it every day."

Pensé y pensé por un buen rato, y luego le dije a Mamá, "¡Tengo una idea! ¡Tal vez deberíamos recordarles que el amor está en todas partes!".
"¿Qué quieres decir?", preguntó con curiosidad.
"Quiero decir que el amor siempre *triunfa*, Mamá Lo veo todos los días".

"When a kid is left out on the playground because they look different or have a unique style, and another kid reaches out a hand and says, 'Want to play?'
Love wins.
Love is still *winning*."

"Triunfa cuando un niño se queda solo a la hora del recreo porque se ve diferente o tiene un estilo especial, y otro niño le toma la mano y le dice, '¿Quieres jugar conmigo?'.
El amor triunfa.
El amor siempre *triunfa*".

"And love is still *working*.
I know this when I see our neighbor Andy help Señora Dominguez
carry her grocery bag to her apartment."

"Y el amor siempre *ayuda*.
Yo lo se cuando veo a nuestro vecino Andy ayudar a la Señora
Domínguez a llevar sus compras al apartamento".

"And love is still *giving!*
Mama, remember the soup kitchen serving food to those in need? That is how love gives. Love is still giving."
"I see!" exclaimed Mama. "I feel better already. Can I give it a try?"

"¡Y el amor siempre *da!*
¿Mamá, recuerdas el lugar donde sirven comida a los necesitados? Así es como el amor da. El amor siempre da".
"¡Entiendo!", exclamó Mamá. "Ya me siento mejor. ¿Puedo intentar?".

HA!
HA!
HA!

"Love is still *moving*.
When our neighbor Bay Aslan pushes his wife's wheelchair around the block at sunset, we hear their laughter float into the air and know that . . . "

"El amor siempre se *mueve*.
Cuando al atardecer nuestro vecino Bay Aslan empuja la silla de ruedas de su esposa alrededor de la cuadra, escuchamos como sus risas flotan por el aire. Sabemos que . . . "

AHLAN!

" . . . love is still *speaking*.
In every accent and in
every language about peace:
LAPÈ, SALĀM, HEIWA, AMANI."

OLÁ!

. . . el amor siempre *habla*.
Habla sobre la paz, con todos los
acentos y en todos los idiomas,
LAPÈ, SALAM, HEIWA, AMANI."

4PEACE

"Yes, and love is still *welcoming* . . .
We welcome strangers and open our
doors instead of keeping them closed."

"Sí, y el amor siempre *acoge* . . .
Acogemos a los extraños y abrimos nuestras
puertas en vez de mantenerlas cerradas".

"Love is still *singing*, little one. Can you hear it?
It sings in the melody of the nightingale's song
or the *whoosh* of the morning breeze, and
when we sing back . . . "

"El amor siempre *canta*, pequeño. ¿Lo oyes?
Está en la canción del ruiseñor y en el silbído
de la brisa matinal. El amor canta.
Y cuando le cantamos al amor . . . "

" . . . love is still *listening*,
to your story and mine, and to all the stories that came before us."

" . . . el amor siempre *escucha*.
Escucha tu historia y la mía. Escucha todas las historias aquellas
que ya pasaron y aquellas que están por venir".

"Yes, yes, yes, Mama, love is here!"
I looked into Mama's beautiful eyes,
and she smiled at me.
I saw love. I saw hope.

"¡Sí, sí, sí, Mamá, el amor está aquí!".
Miré los ojos lindos de Mamá y me sonrió.
Vi el amor. Vi la esperanza.

"I see that love is still *hoping*.
And I know . . . that love is still *winning*."

"Y así entiendo que en el amor siempre hay *esperanza*.
Y sé...que el amor siempre *triunfa*."

FABIENNE DOUCET
Author's Note

A few years ago, my children, husband, and I joined hundreds of protesters at a #BlackLivesMatter march. It was incredible to see other families marching with us, and in the depth of our sorrow, it was a small island of solace and solidarity. It made me think about how parents who are committed to justice must find ways to nurture hope in their children. I became inspired to look for the other signs of love and beauty and humanity that surround us, and to make sure my children noticed them too. These were the seeds for *Love is Still Winning / El amor siempre triunfa*. The story celebrates the many ways love shows up in the world and gives concrete examples of how an idea as big as love can be expressed through our everyday actions. I am so thankful for the people who helped this book come to life, especially Concetta Gleason, Paulina Oriol, and Gigliana Melzi.

J DE LAVEGA
Illustrator's Note

When I read *Love is Still Winning* I immediately imagined a magical thread of love connecting all the wonderful characters. I wanted my illustrations to express this connecting sense of love. With a plethora of communities to pull from, I drew from memories and scenes from my childhood. More importantly, the variety of body shapes, looks, and colors were central to my design. Not every child is fortunate enough to live in a community as diverse as others, but the more a child is exposed to different ethnicities, religions, and presentations, the more empathy and acceptance can prevail. I hope children can see the love and kindness throughout this book, and I hope the grownups in their lives are able to see the world through a fresh lens.

Love is Still Winning

EL AMOR SIEMPRE TRIUNFA